Bharatanatyam (bhuh-ruh-tha-NAA-tee-uhm) is an ancient classical dance form from India.

To those who dream:
Remember you can make
it happen. —SV

For Dadda, who always
had a twinkle in his eye
and a dance in his step.
—KR

Published by Yali Books, New York

Text © 2021 by
Srividhya Venkat
Illustrations © 2021 by Kavita
Ramchandran

Connect with us online—
yalibooks.com

Instagram / Twitter / Facebook
@yalibooks

Pinterest
@yali_books

Library of Congress Control
Number: 2020952515

ISBN: 978-1-949528-89-3

978-1-949528-90-9 (Hardcover)
978-1-949528-88-6 (eBook)

Dancing, in Thatha's Footsteps

Art
Kavita Ramchandran

Words
Srividhya Venkat

Sundays were for dance, at least for Varun's sister, Varsha.

One Sunday, Varun had to tag along with his grandfather to take Varsha to her bharatanatyam lesson.

When they arrived at
the dance school, Varsha
removed her shoes, as was
tradition, and rushed inside.

"*Vaanga*, Varun. Why don't
you come in and watch?"
asked Thatha.

Varun didn't want to. Dance
was Varsha's thing and he was
sure he'd be bored. But when
he heard the *tap-tapping* of
feet and the *ting-tinging* of
cymbals, he grew curious.

The moment he peeked in, the fragrant aroma of jasmine flowers welcomed him.

Everyone was dancing to the beat given by the teacher.

ta ki ta
ta ka di mi
ta ki ta
ta ka ja nu

Varun's heart thumped in rhythm.

Varun had never paid much attention when Varsha practiced bharatanatyam at home. Now he tried to follow along.

Dancing made Varun feel light and free.

Varsha stopped dancing.
"Don't copy me! Dance is
not for boys!"

"Varsha, why would you think that?" asked Thatha in surprise. "A long time ago, when I lived in India, I danced at the village festival every year."

"You know how to dance, Thatha?" Varun cried out.

"*Aamaam*, but I haven't danced in many years, not since I hurt my knee," explained Thatha. "Varun, if you enjoy dancing, you must take lessons."

Varun did enjoy dancing,
but he wasn't so sure about
taking lessons.

When he asked his friends
about it, they laughed.
"Dance is not for boys!"

Varun's spirit was crushed.

He liked the powerful punches and kicks of karate. But dance was different.

Tapping quick *adavus* with his feet, shaping delicate *mudras* with his hands, and showing expressive *bhavas* with his eyes—everything about bharatanatyam filled his heart with joy.

He wanted to keep on dancing.

So, Varun practiced in secret. One day, Thatha spotted him.

"*Kanna*, try sitting lower in *aramandi*," he suggested.

Varun blushed. "Thatha, will you teach me to dance?"

"I wish I could. But my knee won't allow me," said Thatha. "You should take lessons at the dance school, just like your sister."

"But there are no boys at the dance school," Varun mumbled.

Thatha smiled. "Then you, Varun, can be the first!"

The following Sunday, the girls at the dance school were full of whispers and giggles.
"Dance is not for boys!"

Varun's face turned red.

"That's not true!" said Ms. Kavita, the dance teacher. "Dance is an art form, like painting or playing a musical instrument. It is for everyone."

But the girls wouldn't stop staring and sneering.

Varun decided to forget about dancing.

Although Varun stopped dancing, dance followed him everywhere–

quick footsteps on the sidewalk...*ta ki ta,*

swaying branches of the trees...*ta ka di mi,*

expressive looks on people's faces...*ta ki ta,*

20

even the familiar scent of jasmine
at the temple...*ta ka ja nu.*

Varun was miserable.

A few weeks later, Thatha invited
Varun to the dance school again.

"*Vaanga, kanna!* I have something
special to show you," he said.

Varun's face flushed as everyone in the classroom turned to look at him. He wanted to go home.

Suddenly, the sweet melody of a flute and the rhythmic flutter of a *mridangam* filled the room.

Varun's heart pounded as the most amazing sight unfolded before his eyes.

ta ki ta   *ta ka di mi*   *ta* _ _ *ki ta*   *ta ka ja nu*   *ta ki t*

Thatha was dancing!

ta ki ta   ta ka di mi   ta ki ta   ta ka di mi   ta ki ta

When the music stopped, Thatha sank into a chair to catch his breath.

"Not too bad for an old man, huh?" he said.

The entire class applauded. Varun and Varsha beamed at their grandfather.

Then Thatha pulled out an old photo album from his bag. Everyone gathered around to see his pictures.

"There's Varun's thatha on stage!" said one of the girls.

"He looks like you, Varun," said another.

"Look at his perfect *aramandi*," said Varsha.

Varun gazed in awe.

Ms. Kavita turned to Varun. "Would you like to be the first boy in our dance school?"

Varun looked at Thatha and smiled. Then he placed his hands on his hips and bent his knees in *aramandi*, ready to begin.

A Guide to the Tamil Words in the Story:

Tamil is an ancient language spoken by more than 70 million people around the world. While it is most widely spoken in southern India, it is an official language in Sri Lanka and Singapore, and a major language in Malaysia, Mauritius, Fiji, and South Africa.

Aamaam (aah-MAHM): yes

Adavu (a-duh-VOO): footwork

Aramandi (a-rah-MUN-dee): a basic pose in bharatanatyam, comparable to demi-plié in ballet

Bhava (BHAA-vuh): emotion

Kanna (kun-NAH): dear, usually used as a term of endearment for a child

Mridangam (mri-DHUNG-uhm): a double-sided drum popularly used in southern India

Mudra (mu-DRAA): hand gesture

Thatha (thaa-thaa): grandfather

Vaanga (VAAN-guh): come

A Note from the Author

Bharatanatyam is a classical dance form that originated in India nearly 2000 years ago. It has three key elements—emotion (**bhava**), music (**raga**), and beat (**tala**). Together, they blend with dance (**natya**) to give the art form its name—**bha-ra-ta-natyam**.

In the many bharatanatyam performances that I've watched over the years, male dancers have been a rare sight. Dressed in fine silks and jewelry, female dancers often overshadowed the men on stage. And though men were recognized as highly skilled dance teachers, they were not given equal importance as dance performers. Instead, their gender identity was questioned, and their role confined to providing the accompanying music and beat.

Today, bharatanatyam is performed all over the world. In the United States, this dance form is seen as a way for the Indian-American community to stay connected with their heritage. Unfortunately, learning this classical dance is often considered an activity for girls.

Top: A bharatanatyam dancer dressed for a performance
Below: A dancer demonstrating a mudra with two hands

Below: Revanta Sarabhai on stage

op: V P Dhananjayan (L) and Satyajit Dhananjayan (R)
elow: Dancer Raghunath Manet on stage

Boys neither gain exposure to the art form, nor are they encouraged to try it out. Those who do take the plunge often discontinue their learning, either because of social pressure to conform to masculine norms, or lack of peer influence.

Though their struggles are ongoing, things are changing for the better for male dancers everywhere. Thanks to veteran dancers like C. V. Chandrasekhar and V. P. Dhananjayan, men are now stepping up to break gender barriers in pursuit of their ambitions. They don silk garments, jewelry, and makeup to highlight the facial expressions so vital to bharatanatyam. Some have even carved out their unique styles of expression and storytelling. In India, dancers like Vaibhav Arekar, Praveen Kumar, and Zakir Hussain have established a name for themselves through determination, hard work, and innovation. In the United States, professional dancers like Melvin Varghese and Jeeno Joseph have defied gender stereotyping and followed their passion for dance. Today, they celebrate the art form through performances and workshops to encourage all aspiring dancers, regardless of their gender.

I hope that this book will inspire you to listen to your heart and relentlessly pursue your own passion.

CPSIA information can be obtained
at www.ICGtesting.com
Printed in the USA
LVRC091713191021
700868LV00007B/167